KT-450-746

For Izzy, with thanks

HODDER CHILDREN'S BOOKS

First published in Great Britain in 2016 by Hodder and Stoughton

This paperback edition published in 2017

A CIP catalogue record for this book is available
from the British Library.

ISBN: 978 1 444 93110 5

1 3 5 7 9 10 8 6 4 2

Printed in China

MIX
Paper from
responsible sources
FSC® C104740
FSC
www.fsc.org

Hodder Children's Books
An imprint of Hachette Children's Group
Part of Hodder and Stoughton
Carmelite House
50 Victoria Embankment
London EC4Y 0DZ

An Hachette UK Company
www.hachette.co.uk

www.hachettechildrens.co.uk

D is for **Duck!**

(and)

David Melling

Hodder
Children's
Books

Chicken

Duck

Egg

Fox

Goat

Hatch

Insects

Jungle

King Lion

N_o one

Panic

Quick
(Quack)

Run!

Stop!

up

Vanish!

Where is everyone?

X (Kiss)

Yuck

DUCK!

LOOK OUT FOR THESE GREAT STORIES STARRING:

HUGLESS DOUGLAS

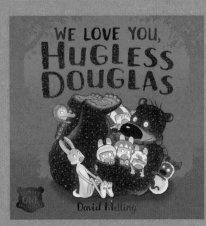

HUGLESS DOUGLAS

David Melling

DON'T WORRY, HUGLESS DOUGLAS

David Melling

HUGLESS DOUGLAS and the BIG SLEEP

David Melling

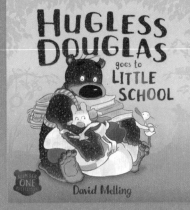

WE LOVE YOU, HUGLESS DOUGLAS

David Melling

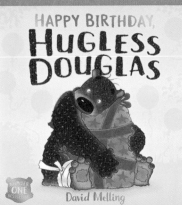

HAPPY BIRTHDAY, HUGLESS DOUGLAS

David Melling

HUGLESS DOUGLAS goes to LITTLE SCHOOL

David Melling

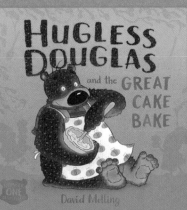

HUGLESS DOUGLAS and the GREAT CAKE BAKE

David Melling